T0158904

WOLFBURN

WOLFBURN

TOGETHER FOREVER, ALWAYS ONE, NEVER APART

BRITTANY BLESSING

iUniverse

WOLFBURN
TOGETHER FOREVER, ALWAYS ONE, NEVER APART

iUniverse books may be ordered through booksellers or by contacting:

iUniverse
1663 Liberty Drive
Bloomington, IN 47403
www.iuniverse.com
1-800-Authors (1-800-288-4677)

ISBN: 978-1-5320-0690-6 (sc)
ISBN: 978-1-5320-0689-0 (e)

Library of Congress Control Number: 2016915057

Print information available on the last page.

iUniverse rev. date: 10/21/2016

CHAPTER 1

THE MATCHING

His eyes are like mud in the rain.
His lips are like a blanket of happiness.
His hair is like a pillow you can sleep on
for hours. When he talks, it's like an ocean
casting a wave. The way he walks is like a
heartbeat in four-four time.
As he listens to music, you know that
he is at peace.
He is tall like a tree, just ready to be hugged.
But most of all I love him; I will always
love him.

—Widith

"In the early 1700s, a group was formed called the Hunters. They killed anyone they suspected of being a wolf. Each group was equipped with two rifles and enough ammunition to last a month, an ax, two butcher knives, a rucksack of food, four lanterns, and a tent that held four people. Each night, the

Hunters would leave before the sun set and start the rampage. Only the men were able to go on this voyage because they thought that women were too weak and would slow them down. But seventeen-year-old Jacob Hannah discovered the true nature of these wolves."

* * *

Widith

The alarm went off at 6:00 a.m. It was the last week of my history project, "The Hunters and the WolfBurnians." I was in the last group scheduled to present. I had wanted to go in the last week so I would have enough time to finish my project strong. I had my dad help me with the information about the Hunters. Even though my dad was the head of the Hunters, I didn't know much about them. I tried to get him to help me with the WolfBurnians, but he just started a new conversation.

My name is Widith Hannah. Yes, I'm related to Jacob Hannah, and no, Widith is not a boy's name. Ever since elementary school, the teachers had thought that my name was wrong. My mother, Mary Anne Hannah, an amazing person, died from cancer. I lived with my two annoying brothers, Sceineth and Zeineth. They were twins and two years younger than I was.

The day felt a little off. Even though it was Billings, Montana, I supposed it was just that there hadn't been any rain since June. I stuffed my deep purple bag with my homework, essays, iPod, and laptop. My dad, Nathan, disagreed with me bringing my laptop to school, but it was the easiest way to do my homework.

A clanging of pots and pans came from downstairs in the kitchen. I guessed Dad was finally going to make breakfast. So I started to head down to the kitchen to see what he was up to and to make sure that he didn't hurt himself.

"Morning, Dad," I said, going through the doorway.

He was still in his red-and-blue-striped pajamas my mother had given him last Christmas. He was humming their wedding song under his breath while making breakfast.

"Oh, morning, Widith. You're up early, considering you were up past midnight last night with that Jonson boy," he said as he mixed the batter for pancakes. Mom always liked making pancakes in the morning, especially when there was a big event going on. The only thing that was happening was my project, which was going to really suck because it was planned out really badly.

"Are you ready for your presentation today?" he asked. "How about taping it for me so I can see it?"

I told him that he was being too nosy.

"I made some pancakes for us, but I notice that your brothers are still asleep so I suppose you can eat and get going to school."

"Dad, why do we live by the Wolf Burn Woods? You know that no one will turn into a wolf. Mom told you that it's a bad idea with the twins. I know you don't want to talk about Mom, but please, at least answer me with the truth."

"I'll explain later. You'll be late for school, so get eating. Don't worry; you will have the answer." He left the table to check on the food.

Nathan does not want to talk about my mom or wolves. I never asked him for too much, but I wanted to know about what wolves were capable of doing. So I ate slowly, reading over the presentation even though I'd looked over it so many times already.

"Oh, Dad, I'm going to be tutoring the rest of the year. Miss May wants me to help as much as I can. I know I have to work, but I told Mark that I would go in around five instead of four. I get off at eleven thirty so I have thirty minutes to get home," I explained.

Dad was playing around with his pancakes. "Not to butt in or anything, Wid, but are you still dating that Dylon boy?" He looked me straight in the face.

"No, Dad. I don't what to talk about this right now."

"Yeah, but I just don't feel comfortable with him. I guess maybe it's time for a change."

"I've got to go. I'll do my homework at school." I picked up my bag and headed to my car. I had bought a VW Bug on my seventeenth birthday. There was nothing wrong with it at all, but Dylon always wanted to go under the hood just to make sure the engine was all right.

The sun was just making its way through the clouds. I thought it might rain today. My phone buzzed, and I answered with excitement.

"Tay, you are calling me really early for once. What's up?"

"Wid, I just saw Dylon with Victoria again."

"Yeah, I know. Don't worry; he's just talking about something—"

"But, girl, I saw them kissing—wildly. I don't want him to break your heart. I just really feel that he's cheating on you with that stupid cheerleader."

"Ha, I'm not going to worry about him. If he wants to break up, then he'll say something. I suppose we just need a break. I'm almost to the school. We can talk later."

"Okay, I'll see you later."

The line went dead. The world had just fallen out from under my feet. I supposed maybe guys were the problem these days. There was no need for me to worry about them anymore.

My first class was English. Mrs. Graham wanted our class to find a book that we could use for our in-class project. We got to read whatever book we wanted, as long as we hadn't already read the book. I picked *The Hunger Games*. I hadn't had time to actually read the book. Taylor, or Tay, was in English with me, and she was always busy talking about other things besides English. I tried to help her with what she needed to do, so, yes, we were reading the same book. All I had to do was print out SparkNotes and let her read those.

After English, I had health. We were talking about relationships—how to have the best relationship with your boyfriend or girlfriend. I wished Dylon was that way with me, but he was so caught up with himself that he didn't want to know anything about me. I knew that being the quarterback on the football team was important to him, but he could take time to get to know me better. The health teacher, Mrs. Alove, had us doing a research paper on relationships. What fun! I thought I could talk about how bad it was to cheat on your girlfriend. Actually, I was going to talk about how a relationship started and how to keep it strong, and I was going to explain the difference between women and men. There was so much stuff to read about, but most of the information was just fake. I guessed true relationships weren't true until you were married, right? No, my parents had been happy, but my dad's heart broke when Mom died.

Next, I had algebra. I couldn't believe we were taking half a week on one topic—quadratic functions, making graphs with parabolas and measuring them. I never knew that Alex Zane was in algebra with me. I had thought he wasn't too smart because of the rumors I'd heard about him. After algebra was lunch. We got an hour to eat or go get help for any class. It was like a study hall but in the middle of the day.

There was someone else that I had liked before Dylon. He was smarter than Dylon and lived close by the woods. I sometimes saw him in the woods when I went out to write. When the sun shone through the trees, his black hair brightened, and it made him look magical. Once in a while, I could see him watching me while I wrote my poems. When I was in the woods, my mind would unravel. I wished people could just sit and watch what nature could do.

*   *   *

Alex

Music could be so many things. It could be spoken in different languages—rhythm, beat, time, speed, and sound. The base of all music was percussion. Without that, there was no music. I wished my life was just made up like music was. Then maybe it would be so much easier. The world looked at me as though I was the troubled one who would always do the wrong thing. Even my own parents thought of me that way, but in reality, I was not.

I was in love with the most amazing person in the world. I watched her as she wrote in the woods, the way she sat, looking at her surroundings. I would wonder what she was thinking about. *Is it something amazing like she is, or is she thinking, like me, that she's a screwed-up person?* She sat in front of me in algebra. Her hair was a gorgeous brown, short but not too short, like a boy's cut. She was the smartest person in our algebra class—well, I could be smart when I was not watching her through the class. Widith Hannah, a very unnatural name. Her father was a skunk. He treated her like crap because his wife died a few years ago. I just wanted to grab her and run away with her, to let her be free from everything. He disliked my family because we treated wild animals.

* * *

Widith

Five more minutes until I had to do my speech—I was so excited yet scared. I was sitting in algebra, trying to concentrate on my homework, but it didn't help that I was thinking too much about one thing. I had gotten halfway through my homework when the bell rang. I heard someone calling my name, but when I looked back, there was no one. I thought that it might have been Alex but decided I was just imaging things.

I had speech class for an hour and a half, so if each speech was four minutes long, we could get through more than half the class, including boring Dan's speech. Mr. Mints, the speech teacher, was the most amazing teacher I'd ever had. He gave people credit when they deserved it.

"Good afternoon. We will go through the speeches that we have, and after that, you will be done with speeches. We will start with Holly, then Dan, Josh, Evan, and then we will end with Widith. Those of you who did your speeches last time can just sit back and listen," Mr. Mints said to the class.

Holly gave her speech on how fashion was important. She did a great job explaining the history of fashion. Once she was done, it was Josh's turn; he did his on basketball. I was not a huge sports fan, but I thought it was interesting. Then Evan talked about a trip he went on a few years ago. I liked that he had a PowerPoint with his. Dan did his speech on different planes. I thought it was okay but boring. Finally, it was my turn.

"Widith, you're next in line. Are you ready?" Mr. Mints asked.

"Yes, I'm ready," I said. My hands were starting to sweat. I knew that something was going to happen or I was going to forget something, but I needed to do this, make it clear that wolves were not dangerous. "We've learned in the past about many major events—the Revolutionary War, the Civil War, World War I, World War II, September 11, and many more. Looking back, did we learn about fighting beasts? No, because it wasn't a big deal. Today, you will learn the history, whereabouts, and other things about the WolfBurnians and the Hunters." I pointed to the screen, which showed the title and a picture of a pack of wolves fighting a group of Hunters. "Let's look at the history behind these two different groups.

"In the early 1700s, a family settled in a house that was the biggest in the colony. The family had a son and a daughter. Once they knew about their surroundings, the children's father followed the children to school. The girl was sixteen. She was very pretty, with blonde hair that fell to just below her shoulders. She had blue eyes that looked like the sky, and she could fit into anything. The son was less fortunate. He wasn't anything like his family. He looked like a bear. He was six years younger than his sister.

"One night, eight teenagers ventured into a nearby woods. That night, there was a full moon and they were able to see things in front of them. That night, they changed for the worse. The next day, the eight teenagers fell ill. They had to go to the hospital for two weeks. In those two weeks, the eight teenagers' lives changed. The doctor thought the changes were normal at first, but then the boys started to look as though they worked out all the time they were in the hospital. The girls changed too. They looked like they were models, but yet they were in the hospital." I changed the slide to show the woods.

"People noticed the difference when they left the hospital. Their senses had changed into the senses of a dog. They could see better at night and smell every ingredient in a dish. Their hearing was up to where they could hear something coming two miles away. Their parents thought that it was just because they are still growing up, but then the group started to go to the woods and wouldn't come back until midnight. One morning, one of the girls, named Widith, found a tattoo on her wrist. She thought that it was fake, but when she touched the tattoo, it would move like a signal. She covered the tattoo as best she could. Her father saw what was on her wrist, and he was disappointed with her. He kicked her out onto the streets to live on her own. She saw that the others had met the same fate, so they went into the woods to live like animals, which they knew that they were. During their time in the woods, a group of travelers saw one of the wolves and reported to the mayor. They told him that it had tried to kill one of the people in the group. So the mayor decided that a hunting group should be formed, and the men of the town gathered in the town hall to fight the beasts.

"They brought hound dogs with them that night into the woods. The group didn't know what to do, so they turned into wolves and ran to the edge of the woods. There was a fence that separated the town from the other towns, and the only way for them to get across was to jump, but the Hunters were too close. They separated from one another and told one another if anyone survived to meet at that same spot. The Hunters found all eight that night. They killed them all within an hour and took the bodies to hang them on eight posts in front of the town to show that these were the beasts that they needed to stay away from and that needed to be destroyed. If anyone was seen helping these animals, they would be hanged.

"Now that I have told you some history, I would like to explain the two different groups. Let's look at the Hunters first. After the night Widith died, her father started to make his group bigger with more men. They trained every night. When they were done with training, they were sent to the woods to kill wolves. After a while, a gene was activated in all the members of the group after they killed their first wolf. It was passed down through the family, getting stronger, and they looked like a bunch of warriors. Their bodies became well-built; they could break someone's arm with one punch. They would also get smarter. The next group of wolves would never be determined. It might be a friend or even a boyfriend, but remember this: they will never be the same. There is a Hunter who knows who the next WolfBurnians are. It's uncommon to have this ability. Only one of the true Hunters will have this power, and they may use it against their friends." I couldn't believe nobody had a reaction to this, but I supposed they didn't care that their lives depended on it. They might be WolfBurnians, or they might be Hunters and kill their friends. Life was too complicated to be perfect, so in their minds, they shouldn't care. But in Dylon's eyes, I could see something was wrong. I didn't know what. Maybe he thought I was not worth his time because I believed in this stuff.

"Now that you know about the Hunters, it's time you know about the WolfBurnians. They are changed by the full moon. Something in the DNA is changed, and they become shape-shifters. They can only shift into wolves. They can be many colors, but the main colors are brown, red, black, white, and gray. The color can signify something about the wolf. Widith was a gray, black, white, and brown wolf, and that signified she was the alpha female. Along with the fur color, they also had tattoos that signified their mate. Widith had slashes on her wrist, and so did her mate. The way they found their mates was, a couple of weeks after the transformation was complete, they would feel a closeness to a person. With the tattoo, the wolves could give out signals if there was something wrong or if someone got hurt." There was so much more to tell about the wolves, but I thought they would get bored of the topic.

"But these wolves are harmless, people. They will never hurt us. Just think about it. Widith left the town alone. The Hunters are the reason for the war." The ending of what I thought was a good speech was applauded by the whole class. I wanted to go deeper into the subject, but speeches had a time limit.

"That was a very nice speech, Widith. Does anyone have a question about this?" Mr. Mints asked the class.

Dan raised his hand, and I knew that he was going to say that it was not possible for people to genetically change into something different.

"Why are you named after Widith?" Dan asked.

Uh, I didn't want to explain the whole story behind my name, but it was a question.

"My mother was a big fan of the wolf story, and she wanted me to be named after the first WolfBurnian, but my father hated the idea, because as you all know, he is the new leader for the Hunters." I hoped that answered his question. There were so many people with questions I didn't know if I could answer them all.

"So, wolves are very talented, they hunt humans, and they can form into a human?" Holly asked.

Sometimes I just wanted to put a sock in her mouth. For one, wolves were not harmful to humans, duh.

"No, that is not how it goes. They are not specially talented. They do not hunt humans. They are peaceful. They can form into a wolf or back into their true form."

Mr. Mints said, "That's the last questions for the day."

I couldn't believe that these people were so disrespectful of nature and the way it was. The bell rang for my next class, which was creative writing.

＊　＊　＊

Alex

I really wanted Widith to notice me for once in my life. I liked her. She was so beautiful. I wanted to be with her forever and ever. I wanted to have the chance to get to know her, but I could always go and talk to her whenever she was in the woods.

"Alex, dude, what is up with you? Every few seconds, you are in a daze. Are you on something that I don't know about? If you are, tell me, because I totally want to try it. Then I don't have to worry about listening to Becca's annoying voice," Evan said.

He had been my best friend since kindergarten, but I couldn't tell him about Widith. He would kill me if he knew that I liked Dylon's girl.

"Nothing. I was just thinking about what I forgot to do for English. No, I am definitely not on anything. I wouldn't keep anything from you, duh."

"I don't know, man. You seem pretty high. Oh, wait, did you do it with that Elyssa girl last weekend? Dude, tell me about it."

"I haven't done anything, okay? I'm just in a thought bubble, and I need to think, okay? I haven't been with anyone for the past few months, and I, for one, want to study for my quizzes, which I need to pass." That was so close. What would happen if I said something else? I really wished Evan would leave things alone.

"This is not like you, dude. What happened? You should be partying until you die."

"Just leave."

Evan left. I hated it when someone got into my business. I really didn't have a test. I wanted to look at Widith's Facebook to see if she was still with Dylon. I headed for the library. I had free period after lunch. I checked her Facebook. *Damn! Still in a relationship!* I heard a class coming in and saw Widith. I didn't want her to see that I was stalking her, so I closed my tab and went to work on my English paper.

* * *

Widith

The library seemed crowded. There weren't many open seats, so when I saw a spot next to Alex Zane, I thought, *What the heck? I need to get things done, and it's not like he's going to do something. Yeah, he wishes.* I logged into my account and started typing my short story. It was a fairy tale that I had made up. I couldn't use the older fairy tales, but I could use the outline of one and make it my own. I was using the Cinderella outline, but instead of a ball, there was a school dance. There was no royalty, and she didn't have stepsisters; she had stepbrothers and a stepfather, not a stepmother.

I could feel someone watching at me, but whenever I looked around, everyone was looking at a screen, *Maybe I'm getting paranoid or I'm into my writing.* I looked at Alex and saw that he didn't look too bad up close. I could see that he had hazy gray eyes with a hint of green. His hair fell into the most amazing black curls. His lips look perfect for kissing. It looked as though he worked out because I could see that his biceps were well built. I looked back at the screen and realized I had just typed what I was thinking. *God, I think I'm falling for Alex Zane, the one guy everyone at this school hates.* I knew that he was in my history class, but I never saw him in there. Maybe I needed to look more closely next time.

Dylon came walking in, and I saw that he was mad because I was sitting by Alex. *Well, dude, there's nowhere else to sit.*

"Wow, you think you can just sit wherever you want, don't you, Zane? But man, are you wrong. Get up from that seat and move," Dylon said to Alex.

I didn't want Dylon to be bullying Alex. I knew I should do something, but I worried it might make things worse. *Oh, well, I will.*

"Dylon, he was here first, and anyway, you're supposed to be in class, not walking around looking after me or maybe looking for Victoria." Um, I probably shouldn't have said that because he was giving me that look, the one that meant, "What the hell are you talking about?"

"So you're helping this person? I thought you were better than that. He is a low person and shouldn't even be here."

Alex got up from his spot and walked out of the library. *Wow, okay, that is not right at all.*

"Really, Dylon, that was rude. He wasn't doing anything at all. I sat by him, okay."

Class was just about over, so I grabbed my things and walked out to my locker. Dylon was following right behind me. He looked angry, but who cared? He had treated someone really badly when he didn't even do anything to him.

"I don't think we should see each other anymore. We have different paths, and I don't want to be caught up in your mess. Oh, and watch out when you go into the woods at night. There could be monsters out there looking for some fresh meat to eat." Dylon slowly walked away with nothing else to say.

I opened my locker and tears started to fall. I didn't know what I had done, but I decided it was something I should learn from. I saw a note on the top shelf of my locker. It was folded into a tight square that read, "Open me when you are alone." I shoved the note into the back pocket of my jeans and headed for the parking lot. I headed home with Sceineth and Zeineth, arguing in the back about who was a better fighter and whatnot. My mind went to another world. I thought about what life would be like if everyone was peaceful and happy. I figured you would get so many weirdos who were high.

I went straight to my room when I got home and read the note. It said, "Meet us at the Wolf Burn Woods, and there you shall meet your destiny." Well, okay, then that's nothing to worry about, just some kids wanting people to come to their party.

I had started on my homework when my dad wanted me to come down to eat. I really didn't feel like eating. It was a rough day, and I had lost the one person I thought I loved. I thought, *Maybe I should just eat so my dad will be happy.* I walked down the stairs to the kitchen and saw that we were having takeout pizza again. Seven days a week, we had takeout, but there were times when I cooked real food and they never complained about it. I grabbed a piece and shoved it down with a glass of water, and then I headed back up to my room with nothing else to say.

My phone buzzed. I looked at it. Dylon wanted to talk to me in the woods. I thought that maybe it was Dylon who had written that note. I texted him back, saying I would be there in a few. I needed an excuse to leave the house, and I got it.

"Hey, Dad. I'm going over to a friend's to work on some history. We have a big test in a few weeks," I said, walking to the door. I didn't hear anything, so I started to leave.

"How long are you going to be?" he asked.

I guess he was in the hallway waiting.

"I don't know. There's a lot of info that we have to know, so a few hours."

"Better be home before one, or you'll be locked out." He walked off with nothing more to say.

I hoped it wouldn't take long. I walked to the opening of the woods. I took a deep breath and walked in. I was not usually scared to go into the woods at night, but it was different this time. I felt like something was going to happen. Plus, there was a full moon. I headed toward a meadow where I would go to be alone. I saw a group of people in a circle, looking up at the sky.

"Well, you're finally here. It took you long enough." I heard Dylon's voice.

What is going on? Is it because of my project?

"Sorry, things got tough with my dad," I said.

The others seemed confused as well. Victoria, Colton, Taylor—Oh no! Alex was there too. The night was warm, but there was a breeze that made it a little cooler. The group looked at one another like they didn't know what was going on. The moon kept getting higher, and we started to form a circle under the moon. I knew what was going on. This was not good at all. My dad would kill me. The moon started to shine on us. The light felt warm and relaxing. I closed my eyes, feeling my arms crawl with goose bumps. Then I felt a biting sensation up and down my body. It hurt really badly, but I couldn't scream. I didn't hear anyone else scream either. Then there was a big gust of wind that almost took me off my feet.

After all this, there was silence. I opened my eyes and saw that I wasn't where I had been when we first started the circle. Looking around, I could see everyone was in a different place. They all looked at me and started to laugh. *This is no joke. It's real. Why do you think this happened?* My wrist started to hurt. I didn't see anything, though it felt like I had sprained it or something. Everyone started to head back home. I didn't know if I should tell them that they were going to experience a lot of changes and they should get ready for that. I decided they could figure that out themselves.

* * *

Alex

Last night was something. I could feel myself change within a minute. I didn't know if the others were feeling like I was, but it felt like a new type of weed that I hadn't done before. There was this pull that I felt, and it was always toward Widith. I could feel that she was worried and scared. I walked to the mirror to see if there was anything different, but no, nothing, it was just me. I noticed something on my right wrist. There was half a rose with writing or letters underneath. I didn't know what it meant, but I knew that it was weird.

My head started to hurt when I got to the kitchen. It pounded and pounded like my brain was trying to get out. I couldn't see very well. The table looked blurry. My mom was in the kitchen, making breakfast for herself. She looked at me like something was wrong with me. *No shit.*

"Alex, I don't think you should go to school. You look horrible." She came over and touched my head. Her hand felt great on my forehead. The coldness helped with my headache. "God, what is wrong? Your head is burning up. You head to your room and go to bed. The more rest you have, the better."

I headed to my room, trying not to hit anything in the process. I looked for my phone and called Widith. I hoped she knew what was going on.

"Alex, how did you get my number?" she asked—really great way to start something.

"Widith, you gave it to me last night, but that can wait. Something is happening, and it's nothing good. I'm getting a headache that is making my vision blurry. There is something on my right wrist, and I don't even know how it got there. So, do you know anything about what's going on?"

"I've never seen anything. All I have is what I got from that project. I know one thing though; I've got something on my right wrist as well. In what I read, I know that symbol means a matching pair or alphas." There was a long pause. I heard heavy breathing. It sounded like she was in shock.

"Hey, what's wrong, Widith? Is everything okay?"

"Sorry, Alex. We've got to get everyone together. There's a lot to explain."

"I don't think they'll be up for that." I ended the call.

Everything was just about to change for everyone.

* * *

Widith

It had been a week since things changed. All of us got stuck in the hospital for three days. The nurses couldn't find anything wrong with us. I could feel the changes in myself. Alex and I talked about what we should do. We needed to get away from everyone before it got worse. I didn't want to see everyone having to suffer because of this.

Alex and I walked around the woods to see what would be good for building a house. Then we saw it—the most amazing meadow that was big enough for all six of us to build our own house. I looked at Alex, and he looked backed at me. I could tell he was thinking the same thing. I started to text everyone to come out for a meeting. There was so much to do, and I didn't know if we could get all of it done. We would have to find a way to get a building permit to build three houses, and all the wood would cost a fortune. But since one of us had a rich father, there was a way to get things done.

I looked at the tattoo once more, and I thought I saw that Alex had almost the same one but just a part of it.

"Alex, can I see your wrist?" I asked him as we waited for everyone to get there.

I looked at his tattoo. It was the other half of mine. I knew what that meant: we were matched, and we were the alphas. I didn't know what to do. I knew that Dylon was nothing to me anymore, but I was going to be with the person I had hated for a really long time.

"What does this thing mean, 'cuz we both have almost the same thing, but together they make one." He looked me in the eyes. I just couldn't tell him, not yet. It was too soon to say anything to him. I knew exactly what it meant, and there was no way to explain this to him.

"I don't know, Alex. I've never seen anything like this in the research I did. It might just be nothing. I'll look for something, but it doesn't mean there's going to be anything."

We started to leave the woods when Taylor walked in. She had black and blue marks all over her arms and around her face. Her breathing was heavy. I could hear her heart racing, and then she transformed into what looked like a giant dog but also like a wolf. It was at least two feet from the ground and had slick rusty-red fur that glinted in the light like a burning forest. She ran forward and disappeared into the woods. All you could see was the red tail. I wanted to run after her, but in my gut, I know that I couldn't. If she needed me, I was a phone call away. Alex's jaw dropped. He couldn't understand what was going on. He was in shock that a wolf had appeared right in front of him and nothing happened.

"What just happened? I think I just saw Taylor turning into something that even humankind would laugh at." He looked at with me wide, concerned eyes.

I didn't know what to tell him. If I did say something, he probably wouldn't believe me. I looked away from him and just shook my head, knowing that was what he needed to know. We got to the back of my house. We didn't see Taylor the rest of the walk. I had to make sure that no one saw her—my father for one.

I got to my house, and when I walked in, there was a tension in the air. I didn't want to be the cause of it. I looked around to see if my dad or the twins were home. I heard something downstairs, like a group talking but in hushed tones, like they did not want others to hear. I walked down the stairs quietly. There were a few squeaky spots that I knew of. I looked around the corner and saw the Hunters' group in a meeting. Dylon was in the group as well, but I thought Hunters couldn't become WolfBurnians. There had to be a reason for this. I started to go back upstairs when I heard the worst thing ever.

"I saw one earlier today, in the woods. It was red, and it was running fast. I couldn't shoot it," one of the Hunters said.

"I saw a brown one yesterday on my watch. It was looking me in the eye, like it wanted to die. I grabbed my gun, but before I got the chance, it left," another Hunter said.

"This means we need to have a town meeting and rules. They are back and ready to kill," my dad said.

"What if they don't want to kill but be at peace with others?" Dylon asked.

No, no, Dylon. That is the worst thing to say.

"You think they want to be at peace with us? Are you crazy? Maybe you are one!" my dad yelled. "You are a disgrace to the group! Your father was better than you are!"

I couldn't see Dylon's face, but I knew that he thought differently. I didn't want him to get hurt or let the others know what we were.

I headed back upstairs to my room. One night had changed everything. My life was gone. There's wasn't anything I could do until the morning; then maybe we could start building the houses that we needed. I heard the front door opening and closing as the Hunters left for the night. I didn't want to talk to my father since he had been rude to someone who was telling the truth. The future was supposed to be different, but no one wanted that.

"Widith, are you going to eat tonight?" Dad yelled from the stairs.

I hadn't had anything since that morning, but I didn't even feel like eating.

"No, thanks. I'm not hungry," I answered, and then I heard work boots hitting the steps, coming toward my room. My door opened, and Dad looked at me with a glare that went through my eyes with pain.

"You're not sick, are you? I don't want that to happen a second time."

I had known that he was going to say something like that. What did he know? Maybe I was sick.

"Having something is better than nothing. Get down there and get something."

I got up off my chair and headed downstairs. I looked through the kitchen for something. I grabbed an orange and some water and went back upstairs. I ate it slowly to ensure that I wasn't just going to throw it up. It felt good having something to eat finally.

* * *

Alex

Watching Taylor becoming that wolf made me want to run away, but I couldn't run away from something that I had to live with as well. Widith seemed like she was okay with this. I knew she had had time to study. I looked at my wrist and wanted to know what it meant. Widith knew, and she wouldn't tell me.

Maybe it was time for me to research these things. I pulled out my laptop and started to search for information about the WolfBurnians. There really was nothing but what she had on her project. But I remembered something about the tattoos signifying a mate. If that was true, then Widith and I were mated for life. I didn't know what to think or say about that.

I grabbed my phone to call her. "Widith, why didn't you tell me that we are mated? I remember from your project, you said that the tattoos were a sign of mates. How are we going to tell the others? Seriously, I don't know what to do with this."

"Alex, we'll have a meeting in a few days and I'll explain everything. Right now, it's not a good time, considering that the Hunters already know about us and my dad is getting really tight on what I can and cannot do. I'm sorry; that's all I can tell you."

The line went dead.

* * *

Widith

My dad cracked down on everything I did at night. I wasn't supposed to leave the house without permission, and I had to be back by ten. I couldn't do this if I was responsible for five others, not including myself. It was time to stand up and leave. I had about ten minutes to figure something out. I slowly walked downstairs into the kitchen to see if my dad was there, and then I looked in the living room—nothing. The only other place that I could think of was outside. I looked out the window and saw three lights and three figures coming from the woods. The twins and my dad came out with sadness in their faces. It was like they had not gotten what they wanted. I walked back into the kitchen and sat at the table, waiting. I heard the back door open, murmured conversation, and boots hitting the hardwood floor.

"Widith, what are you doing up? You have school tomorrow," my dad said. He wanted to sound concerned, but I knew he wasn't.

"I can't bear the fact that I have to be treated like a child, just because there are wolves in the woods. Well, I can't live here. I want to go out and see them. I don't want to just be sheltered because of something that may or may not be the problem. I'm leaving. I talked to Taylor, and I'm going to live with her for the time being. I don't care what you say or what you'll do. This is my life, and I want to live it without being stuck behind walls." I waited to see if he would say anything. I knew what he was thinking, because the look in his eyes told me he was lost in space.

"Fine. If you want to be that way, if you leave, that door is going to close and it will never open."

I was stunned at his response. I had thought he would have been so much stricter. I walked up the stairs to my room and started to pack my things. I ran to my car, threw my things in, and drove off.

Watching the house fade away behind me was like watching the sun setting. I headed toward the woods. It would be safe there for a while until things got better. The meadow was the best place. No one but the pack could see it. The question was how was I going to tell everyone else so none of the Hunters would know? I texted Taylor, "Safe place." I knew that she would understand what it meant, considering she had been there just a few hours ago.

After a few hours, everyone showed up at the meadow. I had a surprise for them.

"So, I think it's best that we stay in the meadow for now. The Hunters have already grouped up. I know they're going to start their security in two days. I overheard that they're going to be tight with it, and there's no way we'll get out of the woods at night. If we have to turn, we do it in the meadow. Like I said, it's the safest.

"Now, I've got a surprise for you. We had to think of how to make houses for ourselves. Well, there are three houses; they're three bedrooms and two bathrooms, two stories. I looked inside, and they are amazing. They all have things inside, and our names are branded already on the top of the doors. But there is a question that you have and it's about the tattoos on your wrists. They signify who you are mated with. They will be complete if you put them together."

"Why didn't you tell us this before. Now we have to be with someone we don't want to be with. There is no way I'm going to be with this guy," Victoria said, looking at Dylon.

She always has to open her mouth, doesn't she?

"You were destined to be with whoever you're supposed to be with. You can't change it. Once they are made, no one can change it. There is going to be a point when you can feel that there is something between the two of you. Victoria, you know how much you want to be with Dylon because he cheated on me with you, so don't even start with this. Now you finally have what you want," I told her.

* * *

A Few Months Later

"Wid, you look beautiful, just like a princess getting ready for her prince," Taylor said, finishing little touches on my hair.

Alex asked me to marry him after we graduated. I was shocked that he had asked me since we were already together until death, but I thought he wanted to make it official. I looked at myself in the mirror. The dress flowed perfectly over me. There were little hints of silver that would hit the light to make the dress sparkle. I had a tiara with a white veil coming off it. Victoria helped me with my makeup. I was stunned to see how well she did it.

I didn't want a big wedding, so I invited only the pack. I thought that it was best to do it in the woods so none of the Hunters would see. Luke went online and got a certificate to be an ordained minister. I laughed when I found that out. I looked outside. I saw Alex waiting for me, and my stomach began to have butterflies. I told myself it was just nerves.

The music started to play, and as I walked toward the altar, my mind started to spin, making me wonder if this was right. After everything that had happened, it was the best thing for us. Alex looked at me, and I honestly think that his jaw dropped. I could feel that I was smiling ear to ear. The ceremony started. I said my vows, and Alex said his. Luke asked for the rings, and we were finally husband and wife. Then I felt sick, like something was wrong. I told the others that something was going to happen. Just then, a gun was fired. Luke fell, and I saw a bullet in his arm. There was so much blood all over. It was like watching a river of blood. Alex pulled me away, taking me to our house. I couldn't breathe. I couldn't believe they had found us. I didn't want this.

At this point, I transformed into a wolf and started to run toward the shooter. Alex was yelling at me to just leave it, but I couldn't. I needed to know who it was. I got to the edge of the woods, and I could see that it was a Hunter, but who was it?

CHAPTER 2

THE CHILDREN

"Alex, it's time; we got to go."

After the wedding, I found out that I was going to have a baby, but not just one, three—two boys and one girl. We hurried to the hospital as fast as we could. Instead of going to town, we decided that it was best to go where no one knew about us. My contractions started to speed up by the time we got to the hospital. As we headed to the maternity ward, my water broke in the middle of the hallway. Alex almost fell on his face. The nurse got us into the room, and they told us that I was dilated enough to where I had to start pushing. First came Alixe. He had his father's eyes and my hair, and he was really quiet. Then came Alice. Her eyes were a misty blue, but her hair was just like Alex's—black. And last came Shawn. He was smaller than the others. I noticed that his eyes were yellow. They told us that he was going to have to be kept under a light until he was one. I looked at Alex and started to cry. I didn't know what was going to happen. I wanted everything to be okay. They put Alixe and Alice on my chest and took Shawn to a different room so they could put him under a light.

After a week, we brought the three home. Shawn was getting better every day, but to be sure, we kept him under the light. When we got home, Dylon, Luke, and Colton told me that they had three screaming babies to deal with too. I was too tired to even talk to them. I headed upstairs with the babies in hand. I put them in their cribs before going to bed. I felt peaceful with them and Alex.

The kids grew up really fast. In two months, they looked like they were two years old. Shawn got better and didn't have to be under light anymore. They played with the others. Victoria and Dylon had two girls and one boy. Colton and Taylor had two girls, and Luke and Carly had two boys and one girl. They were starting to change back and forth from their wolf form. I was afraid that one of them was going to get hurt. Alex told me that they were fine and nothing was going to happen.

One day, Alex went out with Alixe and Alice to show them how to fight. When they got back, Alixe was bleeding from his arm. I ran out to see what had happened, but it was fake blood. I told Alex that he should have told me. I went back inside and started to prepare lunch. Shawn wanted to go with his father, but I was afraid he'd get hurt.

"Mom, can I go with Dad and Alixe and Alice tomorrow? I want to know how to fight like them. I know that I am smaller than them, but I can do the same as they can," Shawn asked again.

"Shawn, go ask your father. You know my answer; it's time to ask him," I told him, and he walked away to find Alex.

*　*　*

Widith

A few years had passed, and the kids had started to form responsibly. There were a few times when the Hunters came into the woods and then left. Dylon had to leave every few months so the Hunters would believe he wasn't one of us. He told them that we were gone, but he told me that my father wasn't going with that. I could feel that something was going to happen soon.

Alixe, Shawn, and Alice were showing me a few things that Alex had showed them. I was impressed that they had learned so fast. There were a few times that they had to be in wolf form, others not so much.

I heard the crunching of leaves. I turned around. Dylon was running toward me with a gun in one hand and a knife shoved into his chest. His shirt was covered with blood. I knew something was up. I told the kids that we needed to form—no ifs or buts about it.

We started to run through the woods. I heard men's voices, yelling at one another that they had found them and that one had betrayed them. I heard a gunshot and felt the bullet pass by my ear. I turned and saw one of my brothers with his gun. I looked behind, and the kids were right behind me. I howled to let the others know that there was danger. I started to run again. Alex came up beside me. *Thank heavens he's okay.*

"How in the hell did they find us? We were hidden well," Alex asked.

"Dylon—they tortured him to tell them everything. I felt it in his eyes, Alex. My brother shot at me because he knew that it was me. Dylon told him. Otherwise, he wouldn't have known he had to kill his sister," I told Alex.

He was frustrated, and I knew he was, but we needed to stop this.

"What's going on? Why was Dylon carrying a gun, and why are the others shooting at us?" Alice asked.

"It's not the right time to answer questions, Alice. We are trying to stay alive. Don't you remember what I told you," Alex told Alice.

We got to the meadow and formed back into humans. Alex went to grab his gun and a few other things.

"Alixe, Shawn, Alice, the people who are trying to kill us are called Hunters. They don't like us. They think that we will kill everyone in town. Your mom's dad is the leader. There is only one thing that we can do about this—kill them. The three of you are going to stay here with the rest. Your mom and I are going out to help the others."

"Dad, we can help—" Alice started to say.

"No. You don't know what they can do; their only purpose is to kill. This is nothing like what I showed you. You and your brothers are going to stay here so we know you'll be safe. I don't give a shit if you don't like that. Do you want them to kill you? Just look at Dylon. Look what happened to him.

"Now gather the others and go into the storm shelter. When it's done, we will come and get you, but don't open the door for anyone else but me or your mom," Alex ordered them. He shouldn't have yelled, but I understood that he was pissed. I grabbed my gun and started to head out the door. I took the others to the storm shelter where the rest were, and I told them to stay and gave them a password. The only way they would let us in was if we gave the password correctly.

* * *

Widith

Alex and I ran through the woods to find everyone else. "Go find Dylon. Take him to the house; he needs to get out of their range," Alex said.

I looked at him long enough to let him know that I'd come back and look for him.

"Don't worry; I'll be fine. It's better if you stay away from your family."

"They are not my family. I have to kill them myself, even if it kills me in the process," I growled at Alex. I knew that I needed to kill them. I had this gut feeling telling me I had to do this. "I will find Dylon. After that, I am going to find my father and brothers. You won't be able to stop me." With that, I ran in the direction where I had last seen Dylon.

There were spots of blood on the ground, and as I got closer they grew larger. Dylon wasn't that far away. I looked to my right. Dylon was on his back, breathing heavily. He had lost a lot of blood. I walked closer to him. "Dylon, it's Widith. Let me help you." I heard a mumble coming from him. "We have to get you to the meadow. You have lost a ton of blood."

"They're coming. You have to run. Leave me. They want me. I shouldn't have gone to them in the first place. They know everything about us, Widith. They know that there are kids, and you and Alex are the alphas. I couldn't help it; they got it out of me. I ran to the woods to warn you that they were coming, but your brother was too fast for me and got me. There is poison on the blade. I can feel it going through my veins." He started to cough, and blood came out of his mouth. I had to take him.

I got halfway when I saw him. My dad was standing there, looking at me with his shotgun in his left hand. He started to raise the gun when a blur of fur leaped. His head was gone. I stood in shock that he was gone. He was finally gone. I couldn't move. My feet were nailed down with shock. This was the same feeling I had had when my mom died. I didn't speak to anyone for months. The sound of Dylon coughing made me snap out of it. I started back toward the meadow. I went to the storm shelter and knocked on the door. "Password," someone said.

"Hunters," I said.

The door opened, and I laid Dylon on one of the cots. Dylon's daughter Tyran came to see what was going on. I looked at her, and she started to cry. I grabbed her and pulled her to the side. "It's going to be fine. Look at me. He's going to be fine. You need to stay strong for your dad. Yes, a lot is going on, but we all need to keep it together. You don't think there's going to be others hurt or even die? My father died today. I know he was a Hunter, but he was also my father. Alex is out there still. I'm worried sick about him. I don't want anything to happen to him, but things will happen," I told her.

She started to calm down. "I know, but there is something I have to tell my mom and dad. I don't want them to go yet," Tyran said. She walked over to her dad, bent down, and whispered something. As she moved away, new tears started to form. I went over to Dylon to see what I could do. I saw that the knife was in deep, but I could still get it out.

"I need some type of alcohol, bandages, a needle, thread, a knife, and scissors. Tyran, I'm going to have you assist. We're going to take this out of him."

*　*　*

Alex

Finding the Hunters is like finding lost treasure; you may or may not. Killing Widith's dad was worth it. He was going to kill her. He was a Hunter. There would be too many deaths. There was a body on the ground. It looked like one of the Hunters. Yep. Peter was a good friend of my father's. "You deserve to die, you killer." There were bite marks on his neck and claw marks on his abdomen. Intestines spilled from his stomach—a great sight to see. Walking farther from the Hunter, I saw Victoria fighting off one of the Hunters. I ran toward them, jumped, and ripped his head off and then a second one. It was like none of them cared if we killed them.

"Where's the other?" I asked Victoria.

"They started to head back to the meadow. The Hunters retreated, besides this one—well, what's left—because their leader was killed. I suppose you did that?" Victoria looked at me.

I had to smile and nodded.

"Where is Dylon? He was supposed to look for me before this all happened?"

I didn't know what to say. I looked away and kept quiet. "No, Alex, don't tell me he's dead."

I looked at her and shook my head.

"He's in the meadow with Widith. He had a knife in him. Widith is going to try to help him. There may be a chance she can save him, but it looked like he had lost a lot of blood. You have to stay calm though. Don't get mad at Widith either. She's trying her best. Plus, her dad died right in front of her."

We reached the meadow. I saw Widith outside, and she ran to me. I knew she would be safe.

Victoria ran into the storm shelter.

"How is he?" I asked Widith.

"He should be fine. He did lose a lot of blood. I took the knife out. Right now, he needs rest. Colton, Luke, and you might want to bring him to the house so he's not in the storm shelter." She looked at me. There was some fear in her eyes.

I kissed her on the forehead. "I'm sorry about your dad. He was going to kill you."

"I'm fine. He had to go. He was a monster," she whispered. She started to head to the house.

*　*　*

Widith

When Tyran told me the secret she had, I didn't know what to do. They were both old enough to know what could happen. If Alixe and Tyran were happy, then they should be allowed to be. They should have waited to have a baby though.

"Alixe, I need to talk to you." I brought him to the kitchen. "Tyran told me about you two. Why did you want this to be a secret? You know we would have found out no matter what."

"I don't know, Mom. I got scared. There was a lot going on, and we didn't want to make things worse than they already were. We were going to say something when it was the right time. I already asked Tyran to marry me, and she said yes," he told me.

"It doesn't matter. You know her dad is part Hunter; he can kill you. I told Tyran she has to tell her mom. I don't know what will happen when she does."

I heard Victoria coming. I looked at her. Yeah, she was so not happy.

"You two have a lot of explaining to do, Alixe, Tyran. Why wait until now to tell us about this? Tyran, your father is in a room lying on a bed with a knife wound from today. This puts us in a bigger hole. Yes, I know he asked you to marry him, but it's too early to do this. A baby is a big responsibility. You are not ready for this. You, Widith, how could you let this one out loose?" She started to get upset.

This was too much for everyone.

"Let's talk about this later. We all need some rest. Victoria, you need to be with Dylon. That's what we need to worry about right now, not this."

With that, we left the kitchen. I started to look for Alice and Shawn.

CHAPTER 3

THE FIGHT

Tyran

After what happened in the woods three months ago, telling my parents that I was pregnant really wasn't fun. Once my father woke up, he was furious with Alixe and me. He stormed over to their house. He told me that he was just going to have a talk with Alixe. Instead, he literally yelled at him. He made it as though everything was a big deal. He knew that I was in love with Alixe. He knew that Alixe wanted to be a good father, because he made the right move and asked me to marry him.

"You think it's all right to just come over whenever and play around with my daughter? I don't think so. Once this baby comes, it's your responsibility to take care of these two, understand?" he told Alixe.

"I know what I need to do. I'm not dumb. I love Tyran. I want to be with her forever."

"Don't get mouthy with me. You are dumb, dumb enough to get between your parents and us. This wedding of yours, you can have it, but think about what will happen once you are bonded for life."

"Dad, we know. I'm not a little girl anymore. I can make my own decisions. This is the best one. It will help Alixe and me. I want to be with him. Just leave it, please." I could feel the baby kick. This fighting was making the baby scared. So I started to walk away, but my dad grabbed me before I could take another step. "Let me go. The baby is getting upset. I need to go and rest. There is nothing left to argue about, okay?" He finally let go. Walking back home, I felt like I was running a marathon.

* * *

Widith

Alex and Dylon came to their senses and made a house for Tyran and Alixe. I told Tyran that it was an early wedding present. All she could do was laugh. Victoria and I partnered up to start helping with the wedding. I couldn't believe that there was going to be another one, but this one was going to be special, nothing simple—a nice big wedding with whatever Tyran wanted. We decided that the best option was to wait until the baby came. She didn't have that much longer. The expression on her face showed that she was getting really uncomfortable.

"I thought building a house was fast with a man like you." I walked over to Alex. He was putting up the supporting frames for the house.

"I can only do one thing fast. Plus, it makes one person feel amazing the next morning," he said.

I knew what he was talking about, but I ignored his comment. He was too busy to be talking about what we were doing in bed. I brought sandwiches for the two. They'd been working from dawn until dusk on this thing.

* * *

Tyran

I felt that it was time. The little one would be here soon. I was feeling scared. I didn't want anything to happen to the baby. I didn't really know what to do. I went to Alixe's mom. I told her that I was feeling pain. She got Alixe and rushed us to the hospital. We got to a room. The nurse told us that I wasn't that dilated yet so she wanted me to stay and rest. It could be hours. I wanted this thing out now. My back was killing me. Each time the nurse came in to check on me, she didn't say anything. I was getting impatient.

"Well, Ms. Tyran, it's time to bring your little one into this world," the nurse said with a smile. Finally, no more pain. Boy, was I wrong. I had tears coming down my face. I was yelling at Alixe. I wanted this to end, and then I heard a cry.

One of the nurses lifted our baby to let us see. "You have a baby girl. What are you going to name her?"

Alixe and I had never thought about baby names. I wanted something unique. "Aphrodite, I want to name her Aphrodite. It will be perfect for her."

My mom and dad came in to see her. He still was mad at the fact that I had a baby. Alixe's parents came to see Aphrodite, and they told me that they liked the name I had picked.

* * *

Widith

Tyran, Alixe, and Aphrodite came home a few days after Aphrodite was born. The house was done by then. It was really nice. Alex and Dylon did an amazing job. Victoria and I helped with the inside. There was a feeling in the air that something was coming, something bad. I told myself it was nothing and I was just thinking too much.

Alex and I went out to the meadow to look around. There was a gunshot in my leg. It felt like a pinching pain. I felt blood dripping down my leg. Alex came to look, and then there was another shot. I saw it hit Alex in the side. I wanted to scream, but I couldn't. I tried to go back to the meadow but couldn't. Another shot hit my leg, and I couldn't walk; it hurt too much. I grabbed my phone and called the pack, letting them know the Hunters were back.

I heard howls coming from the meadow. I couldn't do anything. Alex was on the ground, bleeding like crazy. I crawled over to him and saw that there was nothing I could do for him.

"Alex, stay with me. Everything is going to be fine. Don't leave me."

"They have to be killed this time, all of them." He didn't say anything else.

I tried to form into a wolf, but it hurt way too much to even try. I heard a rustle of leaves, and when I looked up, I relaxed. Dylon was coming over.

"Dylon, we need to get him to the meadow, or he's going to die."

"I know. What about you? You're shot."

"I can wait. Just promise me he gets to the meadow."

"I promise." He left with Alex. I tore off some of my shirt and wrapped it around the two bullet holes. I tried to get up. It was painful, but I could bear it for now. I used the trees as a wall to support myself when I felt I was going to fall.

I slowly got back to the meadow. I went to the house and stitched myself up. I walked out and tried to form again. It didn't hurt as much this time. I ran back out and started to find the others. I knew I was going into a battlefield, but it would be worth it in the end. I saw the others fighting the Hunters. Victoria was the closest. I ran up and saw that the Hunter was a good friend of my dad's, but I didn't care. I ripped his head off. I felt energized, and I wanted to do it again. I looked around. There were my brothers, but they weren't family anymore. I started to run toward them. They looked at me. Zeineth had a gun at the ready but never got the chance to shoot. Luke got him before he had the chance. Sceineth was scared. He grabbed for the gun but didn't go far. Colton had him. I looked away, I wanted to cry, but I couldn't. They wanted to kill us.

＊　＊　＊

Widith

They were dead, all of them; the Hunters were no more. When we got back to the meadow, there was hopefulness in the air. We didn't have to worry about the Hunters anymore. I went to find Alex and Dylon. They were in the storm shelter. Dylon was trying to get the bullet out, but Alex was in too much pain to let him.

"So, are they all dead?" Alex asked.

I nodded my head, and he looked at me with relief. Dylon tried again to get the bullet, and this time, he succeeded.

"I can't believe that they're gone," Alex said.

"You know, they won't be gone for very long. Once the next generation comes, they'll start again," Dylon said, stitching up the bullet hole.

"We'll be ready when that happens though," I said.

Alixe came in and told us that we might want to come out and see this. There was a big, dark-blue cloud. It looked like a storm was over us, but everywhere else was clear. There was something that was falling or flying toward us. When I could see it better, I saw that it had wings and it was a person, a girl. The girl landed on the ground and started to walk toward us. She was beautiful, with long, curly blonde hair. There was a light that hit her whenever she moved. Her wings were twice the size of her body. They fit behind her like they were meant to be there.

"Hello, my name is Elevean Walls, and I am here to be your guardian." Her voice was like an angel's from heaven.

> Looking into the eyes of the
> truth kills the soul
> but when loved ones are
> shattered, there is nowhere to go.
> Tell those who have died
> you love them or say thank you
> Most of all is to
> Remember them.

Printed in the United States
By Bookmasters